The KNISH WAR ON RIVINGTON STREET

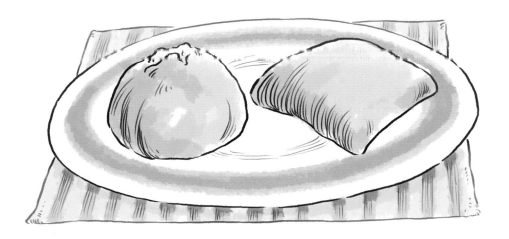

Joanne
Oppenheim

pictures by
Jon Davis

Albert Whitman & Company
Chicago, Illinois

To Miles, who gave me a new title, GG—JO

For Laura and Greta—JD

Library of Congress Cataloging-in-Publication data is on file with the publisher.

Text copyright © 2017 by Joanne Oppenheim
Pictures copyright © 2017 by Albert Whitman & Company
Pictures by Jon Davis
Published in 2017 by Albert Whitman & Company
ISBN 978-0-8075-4182-1

Printed in China
10 9 8 7 6 5 4 3 2 1 HH 22 21 20 19 18 17

Design by Ellen Kokontis

For more information about Albert Whitman & Company,
visit our website at www.albertwhitman.com.

When Benny and his family came to America, his mama baked delicious knishes, round dumplings filled with kasha, cheese, or potatoes, which his papa sold from a pushcart. Soon they were able to open a little store, a knishery, the first of its kind on Rivington Street.

Mama's flaky baked knishes were so popular people waited in line from the front door all the way down the street. For five cents, a knish was a tasty bargain!

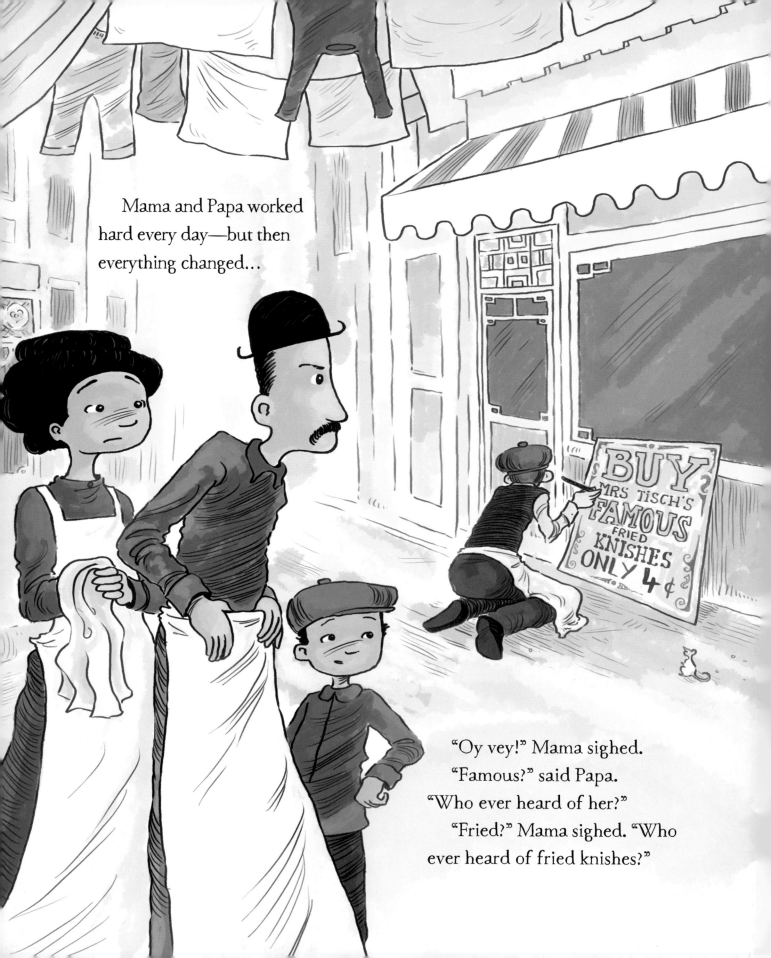

Mama and Papa worked hard every day—but then everything changed...

BUY
MRS TiSCH'S
FAMOUS
FRIED
KNISHES
ONLY 4¢

"Oy vey!" Mama sighed.
"Famous?" said Papa.
"Who ever heard of her?"
"Fried?" Mama sighed. "Who ever heard of fried knishes?"

Right away, Benny ran across the street to see for himself.

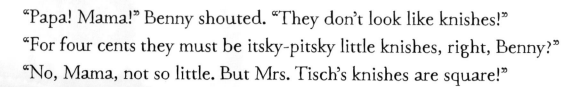

"Papa! Mama!" Benny shouted. "They don't look like knishes!"
"For four cents they must be itsky-pitsky little knishes, right, Benny?"
"No, Mama, not so little. But Mrs. Tisch's knishes are square!"

"Square?" Papa laughed. "Who wants square knishes?"

"Don't laugh!" Mama sighed. "For four cents they could put us out of business!"

"Nobody is putting us out of business!" said Papa. "We were here first!"

By afternoon a big new sign went up...and Papa's price went down.

Right away, Mr. Tisch took off another
penny and changed the sign in his window.

"Three cents!" Mama worried. "We can't keep
dropping prices. Our profits will fly out the window!"

"So we'll put up screens," Papa joked. "Better yet, I'll close the windows!"

"It's no laughing matter!"

"I know, I know," Papa agreed. He was worried too, so he sent Benny
outside to drum up some business.

When Mr. Tisch saw Benny, he sent his
son, Solly, out with a sign too.

Solly and Benny marched up and down
Rivington Street.

Now crowds came to both knisheries, but Papa was miserable. "That thief, Tisch! He's stealing our customers!"

"So what can we do?" asked Mama.

"A raffle!" said Papa. "We'll give a coupon with every knish for a raffle.

"Benny," he said, "you'll make for me a sign...write what I say..."

So what did Mr. Tisch do? Of course, he ran a raffle too. Instead of one coupon he gave two!

The raffles worked. People started buying more knishes to get coupons to win dishes.

But Papa was still worried about losing customers. So he bought a fancy-schmancy piano that Benny played.

When Mr. Tisch saw this, he bought a newfangled Victrola with a wind-up crank. Solly's job was turning the crank to make music.

Both Papa and Mr. Tisch lowered their prices again.

"Papa." Mama worried. "You're selling the knishes for next to nothing!"

"Don't worry," he told her. "Look at all the people!"

Their knishery was buzzing with customers.

They were busier than ever.

In fact, they were so busy Papa decided they had to expand.

He made his knishery twice as big, and to celebrate, he hired a big brassy oompah-pah band.

So naturally, Mr. Tisch made his knishery even bigger and fancier, and for the grand opening, he hired an all-ladies orchestra. Such ritzy-pitzy music had never been heard before on Rivington Street.

Every night the orchestra was fiddling and the oompah-pah band was oompah-pah-ing.

On every corner newsboys were shouting, "Knish war on Rivington Street heats up!"

"Quiet!" shouted people in the tenements upstairs.

"Enough already!"

"We are trying to sleep!"

"Call the police!" A neighbor yelled from an upstairs window.

"So many customers, Papa!" said Benny. "Maybe two knisheries are better than one."

But Papa wasn't listening.

"Benny, take the tray. You'll give them a little snick-snack—a sample!"

Benny was mobbed with people shoving and shouting.

"One to a customer!" he yelled.

People outside of Tisch's came running to get a free knish.

"Wait!" Solly shouted. "We'll have samples right away!"

Soon police wagons came racing down the street and to everyone's surprise—His Honor, the mayor of New York City, was right behind them. Rivington Street suddenly became quiet.

"Ladies, gentlemen," the mayor greeted the crowd, waving his shiny
top hat. "Please, will someone explain what's going on here?"

At first no one spoke.

Then in a small voice, Benny said, "Knishes."

"What's that?" asked the mayor.

"Knishes, Mr. Mayor," Papa said. "Take a taste! You'll see—my Molly's flaky baked round knishes are the best!"

"Don't make me laugh." Mr. Tisch shoved past Papa. "Try Mrs. Tisch's crispy fried square knishes—then you'll know what bliss is!"

The mayor looked at Benny and Solly. "A war over knishes?"
The boys nodded their heads.

"Please," said the mayor, "I'll be the decider. I'll taste them and settle this fight."

His Honor began tasting—round ones, square ones, knishes with kasha, cheese, and potatoes. He tried them fried; he tried them baked. Everyone watched and worried.

Mama wrung her hands.
Whose knishes would he choose?

"It's impossible!" said the mayor.

"What?" said Papa.

"My friends, it's like trying to choose between the sun and the moon. We need both, don't we? It's the same with knishes—there's no such thing as one best!"

Papa and Mr. Tisch
did not look convinced.
"Taste!" The mayor
insisted both families
try each other's knishes.

"Not bad," said Mr. Tisch.

"Not like my Molly's, but tasty," Papa had to admit.

Solly and Benny agreed. So did their mamas.

"Maybe," said Papa, "maybe we could both make a living selling knishes."

"Of course!" His Honor agreed. "In this great city we need more than one knishery!"

And so that very day the mayor ordered a banner.

It went from one side of the street to the other and declared...

Rivington Street—the Knish Capital of the World!

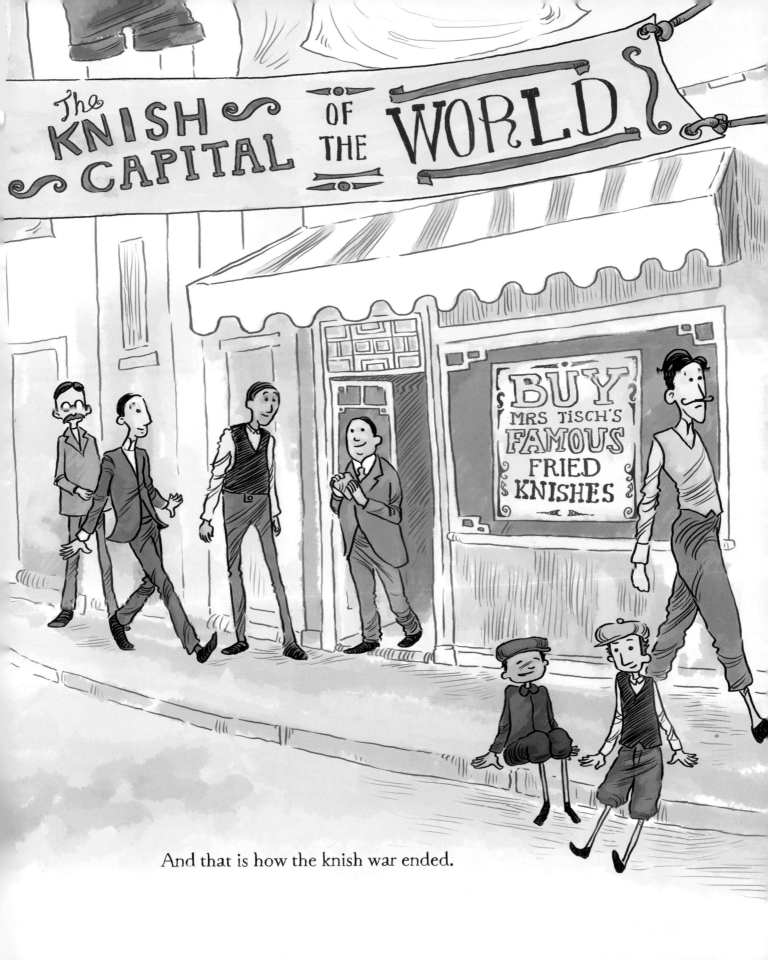

And that is how the knish war ended.

Well, almost.

AUTHOR'S NOTE

There really was a knish war on Rivington Street. In the true story, reported in the *New York Times* on January 27, 1916, Mr. Max Green of 150 Rivington Street claimed to have invented the knish, which he made with mashed potato, onion, and a sprinkling of cheese and sold for a nickel. But then Mr. M. London opened a rival business across the street at 155 Rivington Street. That's when the competition began. Both businesses did have coupons, and one man reportedly ate twenty knishes to get a prize. Those knishes were the size of pies, and the poor man had to be carried home! The newspaper didn't report how the war ended. I made that up.

Of course Max Green did not invent knishes. Immigrants brought recipes for knishes to America in the early 1900s. The knish was a popular food in Poland, Russia, and the Ukraine. Traditional knishes were filled with kasha, cheese, chicken livers, mushrooms, or potato and onion. Today they are made with all sorts of fillings. My favorite is still potato.

RECIPE FOR BAKED AND FRIED POTATO KNISHES

Ask an adult to help you make these recipes!

Filling
4 medium potatoes
  (about a pound and a half)
¼ cup oil
2 medium onions, diced
2 eggs, beaten
3 teaspoons salt
1 ½ teaspoons pepper

Boil unpeeled potatoes in salty water until they are soft.

While potatoes are boiling, heat oil in a pan and sauté the onions until soft and light golden.

Peel boiled potatoes under cool water. Cube and mash potatoes with onions while warm, then add beaten eggs and seasoning. Set aside.

Turn the page for crust ingredients and instructions.

Crust for Molly's Delicious Knishes

2 cups all-purpose flour

2 teaspoons baking powder

1 teaspoon salt

¼ cup cold margarine

½ cup+ apple juice

1 egg, beaten

Sift flour, salt, and baking powder. Cut margarine into the mixture until it forms coarse crumbs.

Add ½ cup of apple juice. If needed, add one extra tablespoon of juice at a time until the dough forms into a ball.

Count to sixty as you knead the dough and work in all the flour.

Cover and refrigerate for half an hour.

Place a rack on a high shelf in the oven. Preheat the oven to 350 degrees.

Grease baking sheet.

Take half the dough out of the refrigerator. Roll it out on a well-floured surface. You may need to add a little flour if the dough is very sticky. Cut into 4″ circles. Put a tablespoon of filling into each circle and lift dough around the filling, leaving some of the filling in the center exposed.

Brush the top and sides of each knish with egg for glaze.

Place on baking sheet.

Repeat until all dough has been used.

Bake for 20–35 minutes.

Let cool.

Serve with mustard. Enjoy!

Crust for Mrs. Tisch's Famous Fried Knishes

3 cups all-purpose flour

¾ teaspoon salt

1 ½ teaspoons turmeric (optional)

2 eggs

½ cup tap water

2 tablespoons oil

1 tablespoon white vinegar

Combine the flour, salt, and turmeric. Make a well and add eggs, water, oil, and vinegar. Knead for a minute or two. Cover and refrigerate for an hour.

Break dough in half. The dough will be sticky. Dust rolling pin with flour and roll dough very thin on a well-floured surface. Add a little more flour to the top of the dough if needed.

Cut into 3″ by 6″ rectangles. Spread a tablespoon of potato filling on one half of the rectangle. Fold the other half of the dough over the filling and use a fork to crimp the sides of the knish. Repeat until all dough has been used.

Ask an adult to heat one tablespoon of oil in a deep skillet. Carefully place one or two knishes in the oil. Use a spatula or pancake turner to slide them into the oil so the oil doesn't spatter. The knishes shouldn't touch each other. Fry about one minute on each side or longer if you like them crispy.

Place on paper towels to drain.

Let cool.

Serve with mustard. Enjoy!